Bath Time Blues

Written & Illustrated
By
Jennifer Marie Russell

AuthorHouse™
1663 Liberty Drive
Bloomington, IN 47403
www.authorhouse.com
Phone: 1-800-839-8640

First published by AuthorHouse 12/31/2009

ISBN: 978-1-4389-3013-8 (sc)

Printed in the United States of America
Bloomington, Indiana

This book is printed on acid-free paper.

dedicated to...
conor gilmore

authorHOUSE®

dreamer...

Jennifere Marie russell

May 2010

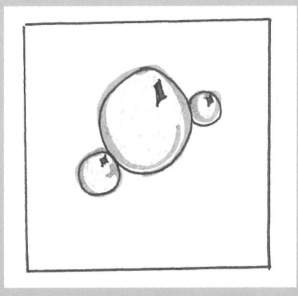

Dedicated: To my four little monkeys...
Elijiah, Izabella, Brylee & Gabriel.

To my Husband Stephen, for always believing in my dreams.
I'll cherish you always.
To my Mom & Dad who I love more than words can say...
To my Brother Christiano...keep reaching for the stars.

Every night at seven...
I'm ripped out of my heaven...

and forced into the tub
for the longest rub-a-dub.

Boys and girls just like me, are sure to plainly see...

Why I definitely despise this time of day because there's no more time for me to play!

Mommy says I have to, but
I wish I didn't have to...

scrub my fingers and my toes
in the suds of pink and rose.

Boys and girls near and across the tide...open your eyes and ears really wide.

Let my tale take you
smoothly alongside...

with my step-by-step
survival guide...for the
dreaded bath-time ride!

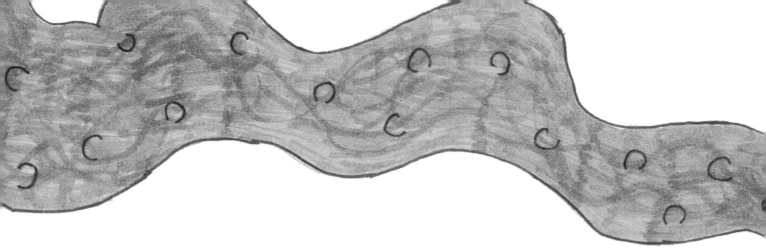

We'll be done in just a while...
mommy tries to make me smile.
I should get my own fair trial...

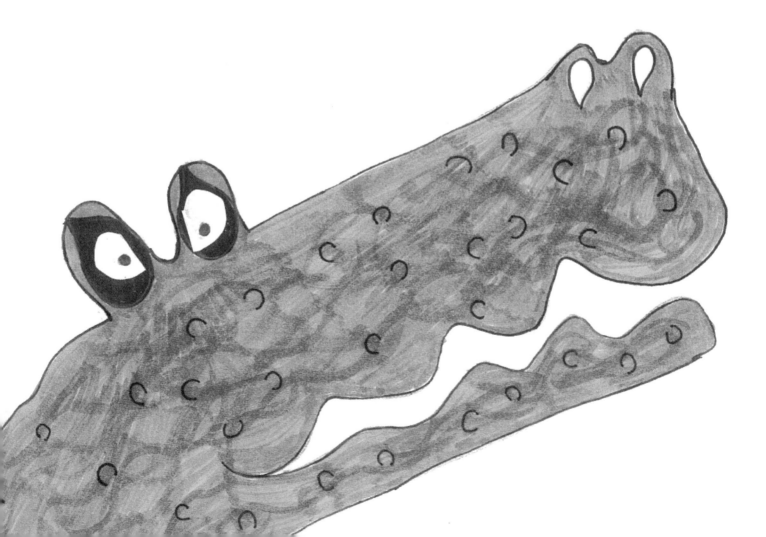

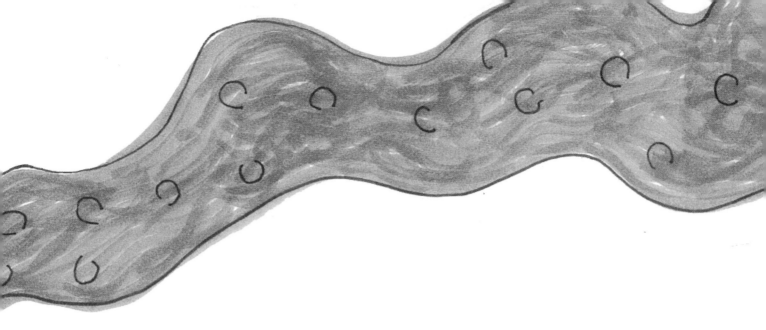

although I don't know who to dial! Complete with a judge and jury of real crocodiles!!!

I try to fight and scream as I sink beneath the steam...

now my hair is soaking wet; the shampoo comes next I bet.

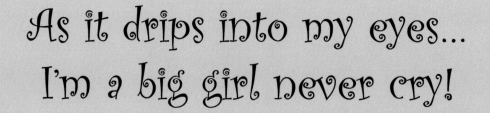

As it drips into my eyes...
I'm a big girl never cry!

Now the suds are in my ears...
as you can see still no tears.

Now tell me if I'm way off base, I'll sternly state my solid case...no need for proper poise and grace... it's genuinely wicked, wicked, wicked...when she scrubs my face!!!

I just hold my rubber duck as
she scrubs away the guck...

that is hidden everyplace, but
she finds them in a race.

It's my duty to confide, since I'm truly on your side. Forget those naughty tricks you've tried. Nonetheless, I've written this tried and true guide... Boys and girls I don't mean to hound, to say it simply...here's what I've found. The best thing to do is to not make a single sound.

No matter what you say or do... one thing's for certain and definitely true...bath-time blues will surely happen to you. We're almost through, I promise you... if you listen closely for another minute or two, there's a little more advice to get you through...

No more tantrums tonight, not
a single monster in sight...

just continue on your plight...
there's really no reason
to fight, fight, fight !

Don't run and hide or throw
a loud fit. Neither squeal nor
squirm or fuss, just sit! Together
we'll use our own brilliant wit...

I almost want to cry! I really can't deny as the bubbles circle high... down the drain they pass on by could this be the end of it... I sigh!

I feel triumphant, I truly survived. Squeaky clean too, I feel so alive!

Be the bravest you can be, and you will doubtlessly see...

Grab a towel and just howl...just jump and jiggle no need to growl.

Let out a great big roar equipped
with knowledge galore...
Feel your heart begin to
soar...because bath-time
blues are nevermore!

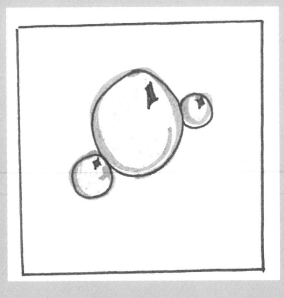

For all the boys and girls
across the globe...can boldly
go and grab their robes!

Therefore, let's try to figure out
what else mommy has in store!!!

The End

LaVergne, TN USA
05 May 2010
181572LV00005B